Mash has a nice, new,
white bike.
He is keen to ride it.

1

Bangers has a new kite.
It is white
with red stripes.
He wants to try and fly it.

2

"We'll have a bike ride
to Banana Hill," says Dad.
"Banana Hill is just right
for flying kites."

3.

It is a nice day.
The sun shines in the sky.
Mum smiles as she
waves them all goodbye.

4

They set off at nine
to spend a long time
on the hill
flying the kite.

Bangers and Mash
race for miles.
They leave Dad behind
as they ride side by side.

6

Dad catches them up at
the bottom of a steep hill.
They all get off their bikes
and push.

7

By a signpost at the top
sits Mrs. Snitchnose,
the six-inch witch.
She smiles a wicked smile.

8

The signpost says:
to the left Banana Hill 2;
to the right Chimpton 5.

The witch switches
the signs and then hides.

The chimps reach the top.
Dad scratches his head.
"That must be
the right way."

Mrs. Snitchnose
smiles her wicked smile.

12

They ride on
for miles and miles.
Dad can't think why
they haven't arrived.

13

He stops to light his pipe
and the chimps
sit on a stile.
The sun is bright in the sky.

14

They don't see
Mrs. Snitchnose fly by
on her broomstick,
still smiling her
wicked smile.

15

They ride on
and arrive at Chimpton.
"We must have gone wrong
at the top of the hill,"
says Dad.

16

They ride back
to the signpost.
Dad gets very tired
and cross.

17

Mrs. Snitchnose is back
by the signpost.
She smiles a wicked smile.
"You fell for my trick!"

18

She flies off into the sky.
Mash starts to cry.
Dad wipes his eyes.

"Come on," says Dad.
"We still have time
to go to Banana Hill
and fly the kite."

20

This time they go
the right way.
Dad gives Mash a push.

The chimps arrive
at Banana Hill.
A lot of kites are flying.

Dad ties a long nylon line
to the kite.
Then Bangers runs
to make it fly.

Dad goes off
to get some banana ices.
The chimps haven't had
a bite to eat
since breakfast.

Now the kite rises
into the sky.
Bangers is delighted
to see it go so high.

"What's that up there?"
cries Bangers.
"Is it a kite?"
"No, it's Mrs. Snitchnose!"

She doesn't see
the nylon line and
crashes into Bangers' kite.

She does a nose-dive
and down she spins.
Crash! On her nose!

28

But Mrs. Snitchnose
picks herself up.
Her nose is very bent.
It's like a banana!

29

Dad and the chimps smile.
But the witch won't smile
her wicked smile
for a while!

Mum is waiting.
It's night and the moon
is bright in the sky,
as the chimps
come into sight.

"Are you all right?"
cries Mum.
"**We** are," Dad replies.
"Bikes are better
than broomsticks!"